The Runt—

A Little Buffalo's Story.

Story by Sue Seitz

Illustrations by NanSea

Copyright © 2006 by Sue Seitz.   28515-SEIT
Library of Congress Number: 2005906548
ISBN: Softcover   1-59926-197-9

This is a work of fiction. Names, characters, places
and incidents either are the product of the author's
imagination or are used fictitiously, and any resemblance
to any actual persons, living or dead, events, or locales is
entirely coincidental. This book was printed in the United
States of America.

Book Designer: sam

To order additional copies of this book, contact:
Xlibris Corporation
1-888-795-4274
www.Xlibris.com
Orders@Xlibris.com

Sue Seitz dedicates the story to her grandchildren, Kate and Gary Z. and also to JoAnne, who inspired her to write this book.

NanSea has three grandchildren, McKenna, Jack, and Caleb, and she dedicates her art to them, and to children everywhere.

Once, when our country was young, grass in the Great Plains grew tall enough to hide a boy. A herd of deer, rabbits and grouse could hide in the grass. It was the greenest green, with little fringes of light brown seed at the top. It waved in the wind that blew across the prairies.

It hid many creatures. It could almost hide the buffalo that grew fat from grazing on it. The backs of the buffalo could be seen moving through the grass like whales moving in the ocean. It was a happy time for the buffalo.

Then the cowboys came with their cattle. They wanted the rich prairie grasses for their cattle.

The farmers came. They wanted the rich earth for their corn, potatoes, beans and cabbages. They had to feed their families, after all. They had to grow enough to store food for the winter. When winter comes, it owns the prairie.

The railroad men came. They wanted the land to lay their tracks across America from the Atlantic Ocean to the Pacific. People had to travel, after all.

No one wanted to share the land. The cowboys did not want to share the land with farmers who were putting up fences. The farmers didn't care much for the cattle tramping through their gardens. The railroad men did not care for the cowboys or the farmers in the way of their tracks.

Nobody wanted to share with the buffalo.
No one asked the buffalo if they wanted to share.

The buffalo didn't mind. They kept doing what they had always done, going anywhere they pleased, eating the tall grass, keeping their families together.

Oh, yes. They ran through gardens, through clothes lines, over the train tracks. Sometimes they frightened the cattle on the cattle trail. Buffalo everywhere. Buffalo causing trouble everywhere, was how the people saw it. The buffalo had no idea, they just kept eating their way through the prairie.

It was in this time of trouble that a special buffalo was born. His mother named him Buffo, which in buffalo language means beloved boy.

He was quite small, for a buffalo that is, and this caused his mother no end of worry. She tried to keep an eye on him every waking minute, nuzzling him, nursing him so he would grow big and strong like his daddy. She tried as hard as any mother to be the best mother in the world.

She called him softly as she waked him in the morning, "Buffo, Buffo, wake up and smell the lovely air, the sweet grass. Come with me, Buffo for a drink at the river."

Oh? You didn't know that buffalo talk? Oh yes, all creatures have ways of talking to each other. Just because you and I don't understand their language doesn't mean the buffalo don't understand each other.

Buffo quickly learned his name. He knew that his mother loved him more than anything. He was so sure that she would keep him safe he became quite daring, wandering away from the herd, sure that his mother would find him, see that he never went hungry, that there was a nice nest for him in the grass at night.

Buffo's habit of wandering away from the herd gave his mother many frights. She and Buffo would go to the river to drink. He would be right there by her side. She would lower her great head into the swirling waters to drink, look up and Buffo would be gone.

Panic! Did he drown in the river? But the river was so shallow, a buffalo, even a small buffalo, could be seen immediately. So she would have to search for him, raise her head to the sky and call for him. He seldom came. Usually she had to go find him.

As Buffo grew bigger and bigger he wandered farther and farther away. He would see a beautiful butterfly and try to follow it. Well, you know how butterflies are, blown every which way by the winds.

He could not resist the birds, the great cranes that came by thousands to drink at the river, to rest and refresh themselves on the way north in the spring, on their way south in the autumn. They were huge and yet they could lift themselves into the air.

Buffo wanted to fly into the air like the cranes, but he could not get all four feet off the ground at once. He was frustrated by this and would snort and stomp and complain to his mother.

His mother was puzzled. No buffalo she knew could fly and no buffalo she knew had ever wanted to fly.

She thought that perhaps she was not a good mother, for no other mother had this problem. She talked to the other buffalo mothers. They told her that they too had problems with their children, but secretly they all agreed that their children were much better behaved than Buffo. "His poor mother," they said.

No one understood that Buffo was special. His daring and his curiosity made him special. Buffo didn't care what anyone thought. He was only interested in learning all about his world. But this was a time of trouble. Buffo's world was on a collision course with the world of the farmers, the cowboys, and the railroads.

Then one fateful autumn day, the buffalo really did it. It was a frosty morning and the young buffalo felt frisky. They ran and romped and snorted and stomped.

They caused a train engine to jump off the track and lie screaming and steaming on the ground. They made a herd of cattle stampede and they totally destroyed Mr. Heinzenberger's corn crop. They ran through Mrs. Wattle's washing, still wet on the clothesline.

They ate all the Village Community Garden pumpkins which had been grown big and fat for Halloween. They did leave the cabbages after only one bite. Cabbages, phew!

The buffalo were enjoying themselves. Buffo and his cousins thought it was exciting to see that great black monster roll over and lie steaming on the ground. They were even more excited to see the cattle running wild. Best of all was the marvelous taste of the pumpkin. "Now this is what I call *massive*!" Buffo said to his mother.

"Massive" was Buffo's favorite word for things he liked. His mother was fairly sick of hearing it. She was not so sure that all this excitement was for the good. All these strange things on the prairie. How could this be good? Since the Two Legs had come to the prairie the grass was going and all these strange things were taking its place —

the great black beast that ran howling and screaming on its special road, and the long line of beasts that followed it, the big caves the Two Legs made to live in, the pumpkins and cabbages they grew in place of the sweet grass.

She didn't think cabbage and pumpkin were good for buffalo, especially Buffo. He still wasn't growing as fast as his cousins. She was sure he was too delicate to eat pumpkin with its hard rinds.

Now, you and I, just looking at Buffo, would not call him delicate. But you know how Mothers are.

The farmers, the cowboys and the railroad men would not have called Buffo delicate, either.

They might have called him a runt, for he was a little buffalo. Mostly they would have called him trouble. Trouble, trouble, trouble.

Although the farmers, cowboys and railroad men had a hard time agreeing on how to share this great land, they could all agree on one thing: too many buffalo. No room for the buffalo. The buffalo would have to go.

But how?
How do you get rid of 500 buffalo?

The day after all that excitement, a town meeting was called to answer this very question. The cowboys, the railroad men, the farmers for miles around and all the villagers got together in the village meeting hall to find a way to deal with the buffalo.

"Round them up," said the cowboys. For that's what cowboys know how to do.
"Then what?" asked Mr. Heinzenberger.
"Yes, then what?" said Mrs. Wattle.
"Haul them off," said the railroad men, for that is what they know how to do.
"How would you do that?" asked Mr. Heinzenberger.
"Sell them some train tickets? Ha ha!" shouted Bob Swenson, the ticket master and village wit.
"No. Just corral them and run them up a ramp right into the boxcars, like we do the cattle," said one of the cowboys.
"That will take a mighty big ramp," said Mrs. Wattle. Mrs. Wattle was not a hopeful person. You may have known people like Mrs. Wattle for there are quite a few of them around.

"We farmers can build a huge pen and a ramp," said Mr. Jessup, a quiet man who ran a well kept farm, everything in place.

"But where will you get enough boxcars?" asked Mrs. Wattle.

"I'll take care of that," said Big Mike Halverson, the railroad station boss. "You can have as many boxcars as you need. We'll put our biggest engine and a hundred boxcars on this train — enough for 500 buffalo."

"But where will you haul them to?" asked Mrs. Wattle, still not sure this would work.

"Well, now, let's see. We just finished laying a spur line all the way into Montana and that ought to be far enough away. We can haul them there and turn them loose."

"But, the people in Montana will complain," said Mrs. Wattle.

"There are no people in Montana," said Big Mike. "Just elk and deer. Plenty of room for buffalo." At this time in our country, that was pretty much true.

So it was decided to have a buffalo round-up party, with all the men working on building a huge corral and a strong ramp. All the women cooked their best dishes: kettles of stew, squash, boiled corn, corn bread, and pies, pies, pies. Huckleberry pies and strawberry-rhubarb pies, but no pumpkin pies, for the buffalo had eaten the pumpkins.

Mrs. Wattle made her special cinnamon rolls, which she never made except for holidays. She wanted to do her part although she had her doubts.

The farmers built the corral and ramp. Big Mike got Engine No. 26 to come from Omaha, pulling two coal cars and 100 empty boxcars. By evening, the huge engine stood under the water tank so that it could take on water to make the steam that would turn its enormous wheels all the way to Montana. By the time the sun went down, the corral and ramp were finished.

Meantime, on a bluff overlooking the train station, an old grey buffalo was watching. He was the leader of the herd. It was his job to find the tall grass, the water that the herd needed. He was also always on the lookout for danger. Something about so many men at the train station worried the old buffalo. He thought that these Two Legs would surely ruin the prairie. He thought he would call a meeting of the buffalo council and see if they agreed. Maybe it was time to move on, cross the river. There were trees on the other side of the river, and grass growing tall and green. The river was shallow. Now would be a good time to cross. He rejoined the herd by the river that evening, still thinking of moving.

That night, the cowboys, the farmers, the railroad men and the villagers celebrated. They ate and ate. Then Fiddler Jones tuned up his fiddle. Bob Swenson got out his banjo. The music rang out through the little village and across the prairie. Big Mike called out the square dance and even Mrs. Wattle clapped her hands. People danced by moonlight until they were too tired to dance anymore.

The next morning, as the long rays of sunshine began to brighten the prairie, every man who had a horse was up and mounted, ready to round-up the buffalo.

The buffalo weren't hard to find. They had spent the night just beyond the bluff near the river. The riders circled around the great herd and then the cowboys yelled their loudest, EEEEYiiiii! The men fired their guns into the air.

The buffalo had never had such an awakening. They were frightened, well, terrified would be a better word. Those huge, strong animals were terrified. They ran as fast as they could away from those maniacs making all that noise. They ran right into the corral.

All the buffalo were corralled and run up the ramp into the boxcars.
All but one.
Buffo was not with them.

His mother knew he was gone when she woke up. He was nowhere near. When the round up began, she tried to escape, but she could not. She was caught in between other buffalo, squeezed and trapped. She had to go where the herd went, right into the corral. Right up the ramp, calling all the time, "Buffo, Buffo!" She knew he would not hear her, but she could not stop calling him.

As she was pushed up the ramp and into the open boxcar she thought she would be eaten by the big red beast. "We're being eaten," she cried.

By then she found herself inside the boxcar with the old buffalo, the leader of the herd. "We are not being eaten," he said, "but this is strange. I should have moved the herd when the Two Legs first came."

Where was Buffo, do you suppose? He woke early, long before anyone, and went wandering downstream enjoying the first rays of sunlight on the water, the sight of a huge trout swimming so close to the bank. Then he heard the noise, the horses' hooves drumming on the ground, the men shouting, their guns, the cries of the buffalo and the thunder of their hooves. He saw a cloud of dust coming from the place by the river where the herd had spent the night.

He was frightened, but he turned and ran toward the noise. Then he saw the cowboys on their horses, heard the cries of the buffalo even louder. He ran to the bluff overlooking the train station and watched the awful scene below. He saw the buffalo running up a little hill into those red beasts that ran behind the black beast. A red beast opened its mouth, buffalo went inside, then the beast closed its mouth. Buffo, like his mother, thought the boxcars were alive, and were eating the buffalo.

He saw the beast swallow his mother and father. Buffo raised his head to the sky and bawled. He watched until all the herd had been swallowed up, and then he ran back toward the river as fast as he could go. He cried until tears made his face wet. He had never felt so lost, so alone, so, so, so, little.

That night, while the train made its way to Montana, Buffo made a nest for himself in a little clump of willows by the river. He had bad dreams all night. When he woke he looked around for his mother, for the herd. Maybe this was all a bad dream. But he did not see another buffalo anywhere.

Slowly he wandered back toward the village where he had last seen his mother. He went up on the bluff and looked down at the station. He stayed there all day, all the next night. He did not see any buffalo. He did not even see the black beast and red beasts that had swallowed everyone.

The following morning, however, he heard a familiar sound. It was the train whistle, announcing the train's return. Buffo watched to see if any of the herd came out of the train. But no, no one came out of the train. It just stood there with the engine under the water tower.

Buffo knew he had to go closer. He was little. He knew he was little. But he also knew he was brave and smart. He knew more about the town and the prairie than any of his cousins for he had explored more. He was the daring one. And now he dared to walk right up to the train station.

Meantime, Mrs. Wattle had come to the train station. She stood at the ticket window, buying a ticket for Omaha. She had her canvas bag, her umbrella, and she was wearing her fancy dress.

"One ticket to Omaha, please, Mr. Swenson," she said politely.
Then she turned around to see Buffo, standing right there, right next to the platform. She was nose to nose with Buffo.

"I knew it, I knew it," she screamed, "Buffalo! Buffalo!"

She dropped her canvas bag, she tossed her umbrella. She kicked up her heels so high her dress was almost over her head. She ran as fast as an antelope screaming "Buffalo, Buffalo!"

Bob Swenson laughed so hard he popped the buttons on his vest.

All this commotion brought Big Mike right out of his office and onto the platform. Buffo was still standing there, shocked nearly out of his buffalo hide by Mrs. Wattle.

"Why it's that little buffalo runt," said Big Mike. "Fellow, how did we miss you? You're the one ate the pumpkins. I bet you miss your herd, don't you?"

Now everyone knew Big Mike wasn't just a big person, he also had a big heart. If a person needed help, Big Mike was the one to ask. You may have known someone like Big Mike. You may even be like Big Mike yourself, always helpful and kind to others. If you are like that, you will understand how Big Mike felt, and what he did.

Looking at Buffo, Big Mike knew right away that this little buffalo needed help.

"I guess it's our fault you got left behind," he said. "So, it's us will have to make that right. How would you like to ride that train?" He pointed to the first boxcar behind the engine.

Buffo just stood there. He did not understand Big Mike's words, but he understood the kindness in this man's voice.

Kindness is a language that most creatures understand.

"Bob," called Big Mike, "Come help me move that ramp back in place. We got a buffalo wants a ticket to Montana!"

The men put the ramp in place and opened the boxcar door.
"Let's pile some hay in here, give him a soft ride," said Big Mike.
"That's a joke, right?" said Bob.

"Nope, that's for real." The two men threw some bales of hay in the boxcar. Buffo just watched. Then, he knew he had to walk up the ramp and at least look into the boxcar, where his mother had gone.

"He's going in all by his self," said Bob, amazed. "He's mighty brave for being such a runt."

"Being brave doesn't have to do with being big," said Big Mike. "Brave is doing something you are scared to do. He's gotta be scared right now."

29

True, Buffo was scared. But he was also brave.

He walked right up the ramp and into the boxcar. He was still afraid, but the kindness in Big Mike's voice gave him courage.

He could still smell the scent of the herd. He wasn't being eaten. Something strange was happening, but at least he wasn't being eaten. The red beast was not alive. It was just another weird thing the Two Legs made.

Big Mike and the engineer climbed into the engine. The fireman threw on some coal. The big train began to chuff-chuff-chuff, blew a long loud whistle and pulled out of the station. Buffo was on his way to Montana.

The train's noise was louder than any buffalo herd thundering across the prairie. "I am making more thunder than the whole herd," thought Buffo. "This is *massive. No, this is more than massive. This is intense*!" He didn't feel little anymore. He felt big and strong and very brave.

The ride to Montana is a long ride. Never once did Buffo give up hope that when the ride was over, he would find his mother, his herd. How he missed them, all of them. His father, his mother, his cousins, even his nosey aunts. Most of all his mother. He thought he was in for a lecture from his mother, but he didn't care. He hoped his father would be proud of him.

When the train stopped at the round house in Montana the door to the boxcar opened. Buffo stepped out on a platform, walked down a ramp and lifted his head to sniff the air. He was trying to catch the scent of his herd.

There, there coming from the north, the faint odor of the herd. He began to run. His heart beat faster and faster.

He ran though a narrow passage between two hills. Down in the valley below he saw the herd gathered beside a lake.

One of the cousins saw him coming.

"Buffo," his cousin called.

"What!" His mother could not believe it, but it was Buffo, running as fast as he could.

"Oh, Buffo, Buffo," she said over and over.

He nuzzled against her for a few minutes, then turned to his cousins, all staring at him.

"I came on the train just like you did," Buffo said. "It was, it was"

"Massive," said his mother, without giving it a thought.

"Intense," said Buffo, "really intense."

The buffalo had all crowded around, but they stood aside as Buffo's father came over to his son.

"Some day you will be the leader of the herd, my son," he said. "You are so brave. You explore. The herd needs a leader who is not afraid to explore. One who is brave. I am so proud of you."

Now Buffo was afraid. He did not know what to say.

"Thank you, father," he said, and hung his head. "But I am so little."

"Being little has nothing to do with being brave, Buffo," his father said. "It has to do with having a courageous spirit, one that dares to explore the world. You have that spirit, that courage, my son."

Buffo was so amazed he could hardly answer his father. Finally he simply said "Thank you, father," very quietly and politely.

But his heart was pounding and his spirit was shouting to the mountains, "Intense, intense!"

The End

Epilogue

In the Autumn of 2004, the people of Santa Catalina realized there were too many buffalo on the island. There was not enough food to sustain the 400 buffalo living there. And so, one hundred buffalo were shipped by barge and truck from Santa Catalina to the Rosebud Lakota Reservation in South Dakota, their original home. The native Americans on the reservation welcomed them. One man pointed out that the buffalo, sacred to them, had always "been there for the Indians, and now it is time for the Indians to be there for them." The native Americans depended on the buffalo. They used the skin for clothing and tents and the meat for food. However, they never killed more than they needed. At the time the white man came to the Great Plains there were around thirty million buffalo. Now there are only a few thousand, mostly in national parks, like Yellowstone.